Hi Race Fans!

Thanks for checking out our newest book. I hope you enjoy it.

In the racing world, some of the words and the way they are used might not be familiar to you. Because of this, we are providing a few "words to know" – just in case. Look them over before you read the book and see how many you already know. Then learn the ones you don't know, and you'll be on your way to becoming a racing expert.

See you at the races!

Scott Pruett

Words to Know:

Hauler: A word used for the big 18 wheel trucks that carry the cars to the race track and back.

Pits: An area, off the race track, where the crew takes care of the car.

Qualify: In racing it refers to the process of determining what position you will start the race from.

Spotter: A team member who's job is to be in a position to see the whole track and then talk to the driver over his radio to tell him what's happening on the track that the driver might not be able to see.

Yellow: In this book we're talking about the yellow flag, which means caution. Green means go and white means last lap.

To our little race fans
Lauren, Taylor and Cameron

ISBN 0-9670600-2-8

Rookie Racer by Scott and Judy Pruett
Design and Art Direction: Glen Eytchison
Illustration: Rick Morgan

Special thanks to Glen Eytchison, our "art guy". Your energy, patience, and brilliance never ceases to amaze us. Your friendship is cherished.

Special Dedication to all the Dads and their constant support.

by SCOTT & JUDY PRUETT

Design & Art Direction by Glen Eytchison
Illustrations by Rick Morgan

Little Rookie Racer's in the shop and being prepped.
The team works very hard, through every single step.

The truck pulls up and Rookie is loaded in the back.
Soon this great big hauler will be heading for the track.

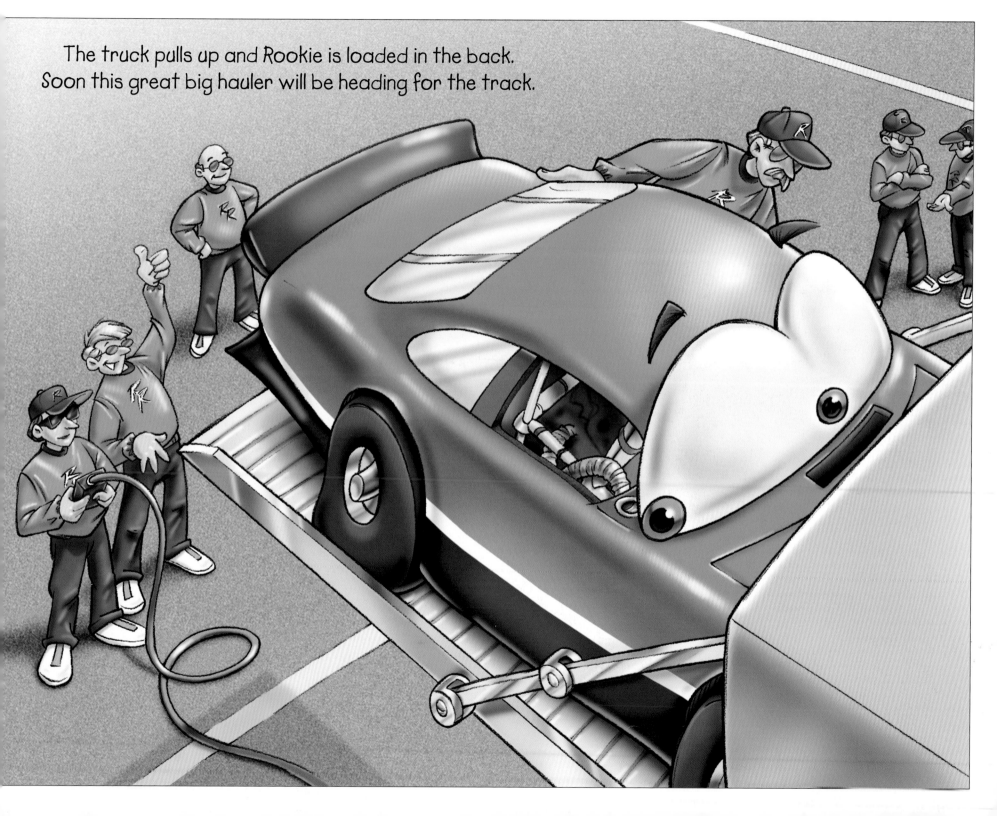

Early the next morning they're
arriving at the pits.
The haulers are parked with care,
so that every one will fit.

Little Rookie's anxious as the crew takes him to "tech". The officials have a system, every panel must be checked.

Little Rookie Racer, on to
the track he drives.
At first he's feeling wobbly,
then he really starts to fly.

He runs ten laps of practice,
then his crew chief calls him in.
The mechanics make adjustments,
the slightest change can mean a win.

Now it's time to qualify,
Rookie's nervous this is true.
He holds his breath for one fast lap,
his face is turning blue!

He looks up at the scoring tower,
he gave it all he had.
Solidly he's in the field,
tenth place he smiles, "Not bad".

Race Day and Rookie's ready to prove
he has what it takes.
The crew has one more look,
and then he takes his place.

The fans all cheer, there are more here
than Rookie's ever seen.
The cars bunch up, the flag is dropped,
the crew chief says, "Green, Green, Green!"

The laps fly by, Rookie needs more fuel,
it's time for him to pit.
He drives right in and hits his marks,
but makes a little slip.

Back out on the track he drives,
he's fallen back four spots.
He's determined not to make a mistake
on any other stop.

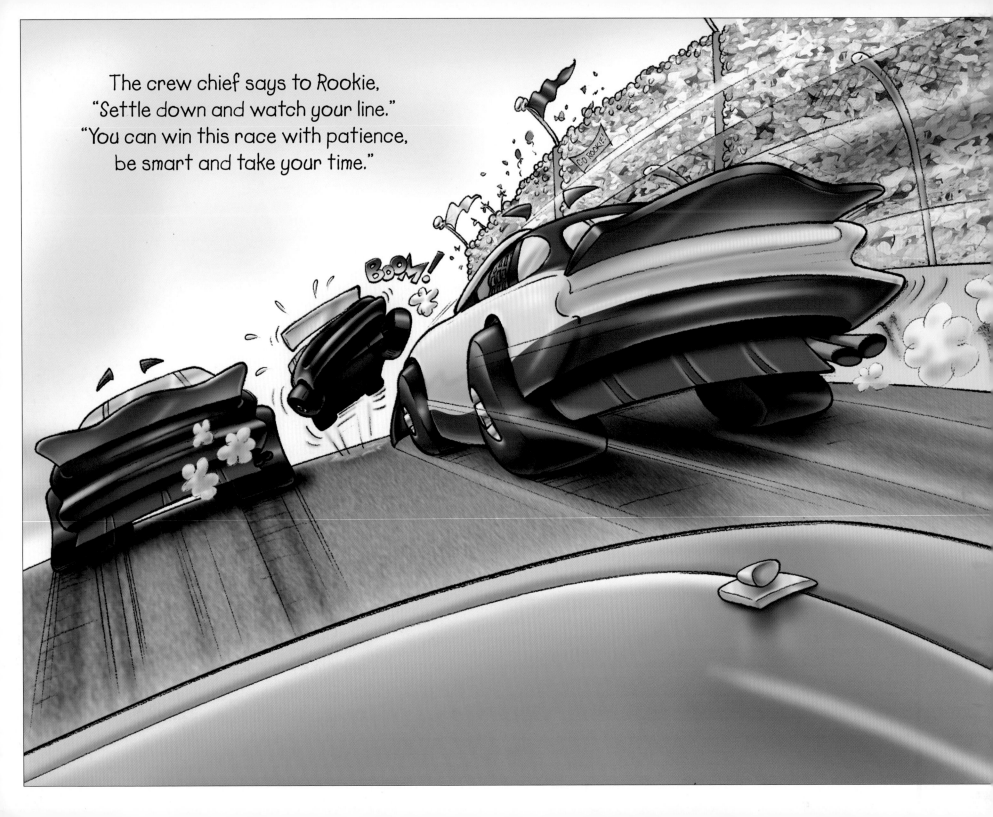

Ahead there's someone spinning,
Rookie's blinded by the smoke.
His spotter says, "Watch out buddy,
another racer's broke."

The spotter guides him,
"Stay up high, that's it, okay you're clean."
You're doing great Little Rookie,
the pit stop's almost here."

The yellow's out and to the pits,
Rookie Racer comes.
Four new tires and fuel,
fourteen seconds and he's done!

Rookie's in the pack of racers,
running at the front.
With only ten laps left to go,
he still is in the hunt.

It's going fast, only two laps left,
he'll have to make his move.
Because he is a rookie,
he has a lot to prove.

The white flag waves, he drafts down low,
it's time to get it done.
Wheel to wheel he trades some paint,
he's having so much fun.

Off turn four the checkered flag flies,
half a fender out of first.
He's hoping his mighty engine,
will give him one last burst.

All of a sudden a bump from behind,
into the lead he goes.
He crosses the finish line in first,
and wins it by a nose.

Rookie gives a yell then slows his pace,
in his mirror what's he see?
His hero, the veteran racer,
he had always dreamed to be.

A light bump from the veteran,
after the race was done.
Little Rookie thought to himself,
"I'm proud to be his son."

Gathered in winners circle,
the team and *Rookie* knew.
If you work really hard and don't give up,
Your dreams just might come true.

About the Authors

Scott and Judy Pruett live with their three children Lauren, Taylor and Cameron in Auburn, California.

In 1999, Scott and Judy formed Word Weaver Books to bring their love of racing to the world of children's publishing. "Rookie Racer" is the third of – what they hope to be – many books to come. For more information visit their web site at www.wordweaverbooks.com

Scott, a renowned professional race car driver and seven time champion, began his career racing go-karts at the age of eight. Through hard work and determination, he worked his way up the "racing ladder", winning numerous professional and non-professional titles, including: 1986 IMSA Endurance Champion, 1986 and 1988 IMSA Champion; 1987, 1994, and 2003 Trans Am Champion; 2004 Grand American Rolex Series Champion; and 1989 Indy 500 Rookie of the Year.

Scott raced ten years in the C.A.R.T. Series (formerly known as Indy Cars), achieving three victories, seven poles and numerous podium finishes. He was very instrumental in Firestone's return to, and success in, racing, logging in more than 10,000 miles of testing in 1994 and their first win at the Michigan 500 in 1995. Scott completed his first full season in the NASCAR Winston (now Nextel) Cup Series, driving the #32 Tide car in 2000. He continues to compete in the road courses in that series.

Scott has also competed in the IROC (International Race of Champions) series many times, and in 2005 was voted in as an IROC Legend in the road-racing category. He is currently the defending Champion in the Grand American Rolex Series driving the #01 Comp USA Chip Ganassi car. Beyond racing, Scott is a devoted husband and father and enjoys landscape design and working with the earth.

Judy "retired" from the field of Occupational Therapy after enjoying fifteen years of a wonderfully diverse career including work in child development, neurological disorders, spinal cord injuries, sports medicine and upper extremity trauma. She is the President of their company, Word Weaver Books, and strives (like all moms) to balance her desire to write and promote their books with being involved at school and raising their three beautiful children. Judy also enjoys music, theatre, training with Scott and traveling with him when possible. She counts her blessings daily.

Glen Eytchison has 30 years of expertise in the related fields of theater, music, fine arts, film and graphic design, including a 17-year tenure as producer/director of the internationally acclaimed Laguna Beach, CA Pageant of the Masters. Gaining recognition for his sophisticated and emotionally compelling designs, his work on Broadway and in regional theater led to design work in advertising, television and feature films, including Warner Bros. releases Devil's Advocate, Wild Wild West, and Columbia's Ghostbusters II. Glen's company, The Eytchison Group, provides design, marketing and new media services to companies like Ford Motor Co. and Comedy Central. Glen has been working with Scott and Judy since 1996. He has designed and produced all of the Twelve Little Race Cars books, and currently has several new Twelve Little Race Cars projects in production. (www.eytchisongroup.com)

Rick Morgan has been an illustrator and graphic designer for over 25 years. He is Head Art Guy at the World Headquarters of R morgan illustration & design, and lives in Dana Point, CA, with his lovely wife Tracy, his first dog, Hobie, and a less-than-pleasant cat named Pig. Rick is an inveterate collector of many wonderful, weird and (some would say) worthless things like flags, toy soldiers and hats. ROOKIE RACER is the third book he has illustrated, either all or in part, for the Pruetts and Glen Eytchison.

Twelve Little Race Cars, Twelve More Little Race Cars and Rookie Racer are hardcover, 32 pages, illustrated in full color, and priced at $14.95 (USD) each.

To order, print and complete this form and mail it along with your payment to:
Word Weaver Books, Inc., c/o Anita Jones, 5951 Sandy Road, Loomis, CA 95650

Name: _____   Phone: _____

Address: _____

City: _____   State: _____   Zip: _____

Shipping:
(1-3 Books $5.00)
(4-7 Books $10.00)
(8-14 Books $15.00)

Sales Tax: If ordering from within the state of Nevada, please add 7.5% of total

Twelve Little Race Cars ($12.95 per book)

Quantity Ordered _____   Subtotal _____

Twelve More Little Race Cars ($12.95 per book)

Quantity Ordered _____   Subtotal _____

Rookie Racer ($14.95 per book)

Quantity Ordered _____   Subtotal _____

Sales Tax ....   _____

Shipping ....   _____

Total ....   _____

Check or money order only; please print clearly; allow 6-8 weeks for delivery.

Autographs